Mmmm... COOKIES!

Simple Subtraction

Bremen K-8 Media Center
Bremen, IN

Written by Monica Weiss
Illustrated by Rose Mary Berlin

Troll Associates

93-20

Library of Congress Cataloging-in-Publication Data

Weiss, Monica.
    Mmmm—cookies!: simple subtraction / by Monica Weiss;
illustrated by Rose Mary Berlin.
      p.   cm.—(Frimble family first learning adventures)
    Summary: The Frimble family performs simple subtraction as they
sample a tray of freshly baked cookies.
    ISBN 0-8167-2486-5 (lib. bdg.)   ISBN 0-8167-2487-3 (pbk.)
    [1. Subtraction—Fiction. 2. Cookies—Fiction. 3. Family life—
Fiction. 4. Frogs—Fiction.] I. Berlin, Rose Mary, ill.
II. Title. III. Series: Weiss, Monica. Frimble family first
learning adventures.
PZ7.W448145Mm 1992
[E]—dc20   91-18648

Published by Troll Associates.

Printed in the United States of America.
10 9 8 7 6 5 4 3 2 1

Mrs. Frimble was making cookies. When they were ready, she took them out of the oven.

"Mmm, these cookies sure smell good," she said. "I'll let them cool and save them for dessert tonight."

3

Mrs. Frimble counted the cookies. "One, two, three, four, five, six, seven, eight, nine. We'll have more than enough.

"Mmm," she said one more time, and left the kitchen.

Mr. Frimble walked into the kitchen. "Mmm," he said.

"There are nine cookies on this cookie sheet. I think I'll take one. No one will notice that only eight are left."

Mr. Frimble took the cookie and went back to his chair to read.

The back door opened and Charlie stepped into the kitchen. "Mmm," he said. "Cookies!

"Let's see, there are eight of them. If I take one, maybe no one will notice that there are only seven left."

Charlie went up to his room.

Anna came into the kitchen looking for her mother. She found the cookies instead.

"Mmm," she said. "Seven cookies. If I take one, I don't think anyone will notice that only six are left."

She took one.

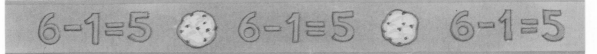

Anna took another cookie. "I'd better take a cookie for Dee Dee too," she said. (Dee Dee was Anna's invisible friend.) "That leaves five cookies."

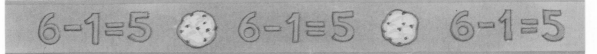

"Looks like I'm not the only one who likes these cookies," said Mr. Frimble as he came back for more.

"I'll take one cookie from the five that are here. There will still be four left."

He took a cookie and went back to his chair to read.

Charlie came downstairs again. "Only four cookies left?" he said. "If I eat one, that will leave only three."

Charlie thought about it for a minute. Then he took a cookie, popped it in his mouth and went outside to play.

Anna opened the kitchen door. "What! Only three cookies left!" she cried. "I'll take one before they're all gone. That leaves two," she said.

Then Anna took another cookie.

"This one's for Dee Dee. That leaves one cookie," Anna chuckled and licked her lips. She ran out of the kitchen.

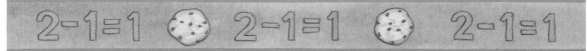

When Mrs. Frimble came back to the kitchen, she found just one cookie left on the pan.

"I'm sure I baked nine cookies," she said. "I wonder what happened to them."

She took a bite of the very last cookie. Now there were none left.

"Mmm," she said.